TOILET POLITICS

AND THE CHAIR

RAPHAEL DIAI

TOILET POLITICS And THE CHAIR

ISBN: 9798748111645

The terms for the performance of these plays may be obtained from the Author.

Published by Ralph Diai Productions Email: diairaphael@gmail.com Tel:08055531301

Ist Published in Nigeria 2003

2nd Impression 2004

Reprinted in 2019

CONTENTS TOILET POLITICS THE CHAIR

TOILET POLITICS CHARACTERS

ROOM 1- Mama Rose

ROOM 1- Brother Stanley, Occupant of Room 1, after

Mama Rose moved out.

ROOM 2-Raphael, Peace (Raphael's Wife) ROOM 2- Nne, Raphael's Baby Daughter ROOM 3- Okoye

ROOM 3-Uche (Okoye's Wife). ROOM 3- Amaka (Okoye's daughter) ROOM 4- Doctor, (also Landlord)

ROOM 4-Julie (Doctor's daughter by his first wife). ROOM 4-Nurse (Doctor's wife).

ROOM 5- Sammy

 Electrician

Plumber

Man, Head of Vigilante

Girl, Patient

Policeman

2nd Policeman

Woman-Girl's Mother.

ACT ONE SCENE ONE:

Period covered in the play is from September 11- December 15, 2002 (about 3 months). Action takes place in and around a building apartment. The front flat is being used as a clinic and maternity home by DOCTOR, the owner of the building. The wife of the DOCTOR is the NURSE in the clinic. Inside of the flat housing the clinic, are 5 rooms and parlors accommodation. 3 are already rented out to tenants, there is a sign board "Room and Parlor to let" in front of the clinic and in front of Room 2. The landlord lives in Room 4 of the house. There is a refuse dump in front of the toilet area. Presently NURSE is cleaning the reception room. RAPHAEL, a young MAN in his late 30's walks in.

RAPHAEL: Good Morning. NURSE: Good morning sir.

RAPHAEL: Em, please I came to make an enquiry about the notice outside.

NURSE: Notice? Which notice?

RAPHAEL: I mean the room and parlor to let. NURSE: Oh, that one, excuse me (As she turns to

enter the inner room in the clinic, Doctor comes out) Doctor this man is asking after the vacancy for room and parlor.

RAPHAEL: Good morning sir.

DOCTOR: Good morning. How may I help you? RAPHAEL: I want accommodation, can I see what

you have?

DOCTOR: (To the Nurse) let me have the keys to the place.

NURSE: Picks up a bunch of keys from the table and gives it to him.

DOCTOR: (To Raphael) Please follow me. (They go to room 2, and enter inside.

 NURSE:(Continues in her work, singing the tune)This is the day that the Lord has made I will rejoice and be glad in it. (As she completes, then DOCTOR and RAPHAEL come out from Room 2.)

RAPHAEL: There is some work to be done. DOCTOR: No problem, the bricklayers will just

patch it up.

RAPHAEL: How about the kitchen? DOCTOR: Come let me show you?

They walk toward the entrance of room 5 and enter.

MAMA ROSE comes out from room 1. She is a woman of about 44, thin and not exactly one who can be classified as beautiful, she has on one hand a soap dish which she drops on the floor and on the other hand a bucket. She has a towel wrapped round her neck. She sings, 'It must be permanent'. She goes off stage with the bucket. DOCTOR and RAPHAEL come out of the kitchen. RAPHAEL: The space is too small, besides it's in front

of somebody's room, I don't like trouble.

DOCTOR: There will be no trouble. That's where everybody cooks, or if you like, you can do it in front of your room.

RAPHAEL: What about these? (Pointing to the fallen bricks)

DOCTOR: Oh that, the rains brought them down,

the kind of rain we experienced this year, we have never experienced that kind before. Never mind, I know what to do, I shall use metal to reinforce it, so that it does not fall again.

RAPHAEL: The bathroom, let me take a look. (He turns to go there.)

DOCTOR: Excuse me, my attention is needed in the clinic (leaves).

RAPHAEL: (Opens the bathroom door, looks in, then sees the toilet tries to open it, it is padlocked, so he turns around and walks toward the clinics.)

MAMA ROSE: (Enters with her bucket of water still singing) It must be permanent.

RAPHAEL: (meets MAMA ROSE in front of room 1) Good morning Madam.

MAMA ROSE: Good morning.

RAPHAEL;   Madam please don't be offended, when it rains, does water enter inside the house?

MAMA ROSE: It does not enter my room, but the parlor, yes.

RAPHAEL: Thank you.

MAMA ROSE; Oga, why do you want to enter a place like this?

RAPHAEL: It is because it is not face-me-I-face-You, that's why.

MAMA ROSE: You sure?? RAPHAEL: Condition.

MAMA ROSE: What kind of condition, I see you are decent looking.

RAPHAEL: It's a long story.

MAMA ROSE: Tell me, I like hearing stories. RAPHAEL: Not my kind, Thank you. (Walks away) MAMA ROSE: See me o, did I say something wrong?

(Picks up her soap dish) this my mouth

self you have spoilt everything. RAPHAEL: (Exit Stage).

MAMA ROSE: God save me. (Carries her bucket and head toward the bathroom singing) 'I

have seen the downfall of Satan, glory be to God' (Enter the bathroom)

FADE TO BLACK

SCENE TWO:

Evening of the same day RAPHAEL is in the clinic to pay the rent, Doctor is sitting on top of the reception table, as RAPHAEL brings out the money, DOCTOR starts counting.

RAPHAEL: Please, I will like to see that those things I

pointed out are taken care of. DOCTOR: No problem (Completes the counting

and looks up) Can I see your I.D. Card? RAPHAEL: (Brings out his identification card and

hands it over.)

DOCTOR: (Reading it, as he writes receipt for him) Mr. Raphael, are you a writer?

RAPHAEL: Yes.

DOCTOR: (Handing the I.D card to RAPHAEL) What do you write?

RAPHAEL: Drama for stage and home video. DOCTOR: Now Mr. Raphael (Puts the money away)

the conditions for staying in this house

are these, when your rent expires you will be paying every six months. You will manage the small kitchen with the rest of the people, so I expect you to cooperate with us in this yard. Women bring too much palaver; don't take everything they say to heart. Are you a Christian or Muslim?

RAPHAEL: A Christian.

DOCTOR: Don't be offended, I just asked to know what to say next. We must tolerate each other no matter our religious leanings. See me, I am a Christian, my people are Muslims, they tolerate me, I show them love. If you need anything, let me know.

RAPHAEL: Thank you.

DOCTOR: (Gives the keys to RAPHAEL) I will send you the agreement paper later.

RAPHAEL: Thank you (leaves the clinic and enters room 2.)

DOCTOR: Collects the money from where he kept it and enters into the clinic.

MAMA ROSE (Comes out from room 1, singing) On the Mountain, in the valley, on the land and in the sea, alleluia, the LORD is my portion in the land of the living. (Spreads some clothes on the block in front of room 2.)

RAPHAEL: (Comes out, sees her and greets) Well done madam.

MAMA ROSE: Thank you my brother. Have you paid? RAPHAEL: Yes.

MAMA ROSE: This is a useless compound, there is no cooperation.

RAPHAEL: Is that so?

MAMA ROSE: There is no toilet. The toilet blocked for over 7 months and he refused to repair it.

I see you are a Christian. That is why I am telling you this. You have to pray very well. People don't make progress here. He will wait for you when your rent

expires, then he will increase your rent so much that you will protest. If the person refuses, he will give him quit notice so that he can collect rent of another 2 years instead of 6 months.

RAPHAEL: But Madam, why didn't you tell me all these earlier before I paid.

MAMA ROSE: It's what you asked that I answered

RAPHAEL: It's true. I am going to ask the landlord about the toilet (leaves).

MAMA ROSE: Don't tell him I told you.

RAPHAEL: (Enters the clinic and sees the Doctor coming out of the inner chamber) Excuse me Doctor.

DOCTOR: I hope no problem.

RAPHAEL: I notice all electrical fittings have been disconnected.

DOCTOR: You can find an electrician to do it for you.

RAPHAEL: I thought all these are supposed to be in place before I move in.

DOCTOR: It is a minor thing, we will look for an electrician to fix it.

RAPHAEL: Em, also I have not seen the toilet, it was locked when I checked.

DOCTOR: Toilet, toilet, there's a minor fault we'll fix it this weekend or early next week.

RAPHAEL: If you say so, I shall have to delay my moving in, to enable you put things right.

DOCTOR: This weekend everything will be alright, please don't let it prevent you from moving your things.

SCENE 3:

RAPHAEL and his family have just packed into their room and parlor. RAPHAEL hangs a curtain on his door and enters inside.

MAMA ROSE: (Comes out from her room singing) JESUS is a Winner man, Winner man, JESUS is a Winner man, winner man all the time.

RAPHAEL: (Emerges from his room with a bucket and a small rubber container used for drawing water from the well he heads toward the clinic.)

MAMA ROSE: (To RAPHAEL) Brother don't fetch from that well, the water in the well there is not clean, it's the well over there that we use, it's cleaner.

RAPHAEL: Thank you. (Remembers that the rubber container is leaking underneath decides to do as the lady says, to prevent him from splashing so much water on the floor. As RAPHAEL leaves the stage to go and fetch water JULIE, DOCTOR's teenage daughter who all this while has been in front of room 4 and obviously heard what   transpired between RAPHAEL and MAMA ROSE, now rushes forward shouting.)

JULIE: This mad woman you have started again.

MAMA ROSE: It's your mother that is mad.

JULIE: Good for nothing woman, when you have finished consuming your ogogoro that

you sell you come here to talk nonsense.(The noise attracts PEACE, RAPHAEL'S wife from the room, DOCTOR'S wife NURSE comes out while RAPHAEL comes on stage with his bucket of water and container.

PEACE: Madam, what is it?

MAMA ROSE: Don't mind this useless girl. JULIE: It's your children that are useless. PEACE: (To Julie) You, take it easy.

JULIE: See how she is insulting me.

NURSE: Julie, leave her alone, you know how she behaves.

RAPHAEL: What is going on here?

JULIE: She said our well is polluted that you should not fetch from it.

RAPHAEL: (Smiles) Oh that! Is that what is causing this palaver? She advised me alright, but the reason I didn't fetch from the well is because of this my container, it is leaking, I don't want it to wet the floor.

MAMA ROSE: See me, see trouble, if I see truth, shouldn't I say it?

NURSE: What is your business, busybody.

MAMA ROSE: Eh! Eh! Nobody called you in this matter, you cannot control small girl like this you come to open your mouth for me.

JULIE: Me small girl?

NURSE: You are sick (To MAMA ROSE) RAPHAEL and wife are at a loss on what to do, they observe them for a while.

MAMA ROSE: All of you are sick, your father, mother, you all. Who in his right mind will stay in this place?

JULIE: It pains you because my dad gave you quit notice.

MAMA ROSE: For a house he did not build. JULIE: He built it with his money.

MAMA ROSE: Shut up, what do you know, it is your grandfather's
        house, can that your hopeless father mould block? He built it
with his own money my foot.

NURSE: (To RAPHAEL) Sir, you see how she is insulting my oga?

RAPHAEL: (To NURSE) Take it easy. (To MAMA ROSE) woman control
your tongue (To JULIE and MAMA ROSE) are you people not ashamed of
yourselves?

MAMA ROSE: Why should I be ashamed, after all I did not steal in the
church as she did (To Julie) Thief.

NURSE: Look mind what you say. MAMA ROSE: Is it a lie? Thief.

RAPHAEL and his wife look at each other. There's momentary silence,
RAPHAEL capitalizes on it.

RAPHAEL: (To JULIE and NURSE) it's alright, go inside. (To MAMA ROSE)
It is enough.

MAMA ROSE: Thank you sir, you should have allowed me to complete
her life history.

JULIE: You will see (leaving)

MAMA ROSE: I see nothing, shameless girl.

JULIE: (To RAPHAEL) You see she has started again

PEACE: (Disgusted with the whole scenario.) Darling, leave these ones
alone. It's like trouble is their middle name (Exit)

RAPHAEL: (To Nurse) Take her away now.

MAMA ROSE: Silly girl that is not up to my daughter. NURSE: This one will not keep quiet.

JULIE: That your daughter with two left legs? RAPHAEL: Oh! This is getting out of hand (Shouts)

shut up, all of you, shut up! Ah, this is my first day in this compound what a reception. I am most disgusted with this display of shame, is this how you people behave?

ALL: Sorry Sir.

RAPHAEL: Enough is enough, see how people are looking and laughing at us. Now all of you go inside.

NURSE: (Drags JULIE inside, RAPHAEL enters his room, while MAMA ROSE starts singing.)

MAMA ROSE: JESUS you are a winner man.

FADE SCENE 4:

Early in the morning, PEACE comes out from their room and head straight for the toilet, she gets there and discovers that there is a padlock on the door, she goes to room 4, knocks and NURSE opens the door.

PEACE: Good morning. NURSE: Good morning.

PEACE: Please I want to use the toilet, I see that it is locked.

NURSE: Please wait let me call Doctor (enters inside and DOCTOR emerges)

PEACE: Good morning Doctor. DOCTOR: Good morning.

PEACE: Please I want to use the toilet and the place is locked.

DOCTOR: Em, no problem, you can come and use the one in the clinic.

He moves, she follows him, as they get to the clinic, DOCTOR points to a door, and enters his own office. There is a girl waiting in the reception, as soon as the DOCTOR enters his office, the girl rises and follows him inside. Meanwhile PEACE enters the toilet and comes out covering her nose, she goes toward her

apartment and sees MAMA ROSE coming out from the bathroom with a cellophane bag which she flings carelessly into the refuse dump in the toilet.

PEACE: Good morning.

MAMA ROSE: Good morning my sister, have you woken up this morning?

PEACE: Yes, please how do you people cope with the toilet?

MAMA ROSE: We do it in the bathroom and throw it yonder. (Pointing at the refuse heap.)

PEACE: Is this man really a Doctor?

SAMMY: Comes out of the door leading to room 5 and enters the bathroom.

MAMA ROSE: I keep asking myself the same question.

For over 7 months this toilet blocked, we contributed N3,500 out of the N5,000 charged to do the work, we asked him to bring the balance, no way. He wants the tenants to do everything but he forgets that what his family and clinic deposit there, is more than double the tenants own.

PEACE: So what happened? MAMA ROSE: We refused.

(Just then, there is a shout from the clinic, like someone in pain.)

PEACE: (Shocked) What's that?

MAMA ROSE: We hear it from time to time, that is what he does.

PEACE: Who?

MAMA ROSE: Him (Pointing to the clinic) abortion for all these girls.

PEACE: That is terrible it's a crime against God and man...and he has a daughter.

MAMA ROSE: Go and tell him that.

SAMMY: Comes out of the bathroom with his bucket in his right hand, while he has a cellophane bag in his left, he flings it too into the refuse heap.

MAMA ROSE: (Sees SAMMY) Ask Sammy. SAMMY: Una Good Morning.

PEACE: Morning.

MAMA ROSE: I was telling her what we have passed through since the toilet became full.

SAMMY: The toilet is not filled. The pipe needs clearing, but the man does not want to hear.

PEACE: This is bad.

The girl comes out from the clinic in pains, but braces up as she sees the two women standing. MAMA ROSE sees her as she comes out and beckons on PEACE to see. DOCTOR comes out of the clinic and looks around.

MAMA ROSE: (Starts singing) Satan shame unto you,

Alleluia (Enters her room.)

PEACE: Contemplates what next to do, head toward the DOCTOR.

DOCTOR: (Sensing confrontation) Madam, don't worry, everything will be alright. Don't listen to what anybody says especially that woman, she has mental problem.

PEACE: Why then did you give her your house? DOCTOR: Actually I don't have anything to do with her. Her brother rented the place for her. When she started giving too much heat, he advised that when her rent expires, I should give her quit notice and that is what I have done. She will be leaving in three days time.

PEACE: But Doctor, this idea of using the bathroom and disposing of waste in this manner (points to the refuse dump) is not good for the environment especially the hospital.

DOCTOR: I know. I have sent Sammy to get sewage disposal van, as soon as that woman leaves everything will be alright.

PEACE: I hear money is the issue.

DOCTOR: You have started hearing. Don't believe anything these ones tell you. It is due to their   non co-operation   that things degenerated to this level, they all want to show sense.

PEACE: (Shakes her head) Too bad.

DOCTOR: Relax, if there's any problem, just let me know.

PEACE: There's no light in our apartment. DOCTOR: Your husband told me. I will help call an

electrician, but if you see one before me, let him do it, no problem.

PEACE: Okay (enters her room.)

FADE SCENE 5:

MAMA ROSE is moving out of the house, some of her things are outside, she picks up her box and is about to leave when RAPHAEL walks in.

RAPHAEL: Madam, so it is true you are leaving.

MAMA ROSE: Yes O, this is not a good compound. Like I told you my brother, pray very well, so that your own will be different, there is nothing our God cannot do (Starts singing) "There is nothing our God cannot do" (Leaves)

NURSE: (Enters with a man, an electrician. She calls RAPHAEL as he is about entering his room) Excuse me Sir.

RAPHAEL: Yes?

NURSE: I have called the electrician to help you connect your light.

RAPHAEL: Thank you, please come in (They enter, AMAKA, OKOYE's daughter in room 3 dressed in school uniform comes back, opens their door and enters inside. RAPHAEL,electrician and NURSE come out from room 2)

RAPHAEL; Is that so? NURSE: Yes O.

RAPHAEL: How regular is light here?

NURSE: They ration it, One day on, One day off, even our day on, is not the full day.

RAPHAEL: You cannot complain because you don't pay. This country self. God save us.

NURSE: Amen. Excuse me (Leaves for the clinic AMAKA comes out from room 3 and sees RAPHAEL standing, he is obviously thinking about their just concluded conversation.)

AMAKA: Brother, good afternoon. RAPAHAEL: Afternoon, how are you? AMAKA: Fine sir.

RAPHAEL: How are your parents, I hardly see them. AMAKA: They are fine, they have gone to work. RAPHAEL: What kind of work does your dad and

mum do?

AMAKA: My father sells electronic and my mother sells food at Alaba.

RAPHAEL: Why don't you go to your mum's shop when you close from school is it not

near? AMAKA: It is near.

RAPHAEL: It is risky for a young girl like you to be left alone just like that. I will speak to your dad about it. Have you eaten?

AMAKA: No sir, there is nothing at home

RAPHAEL: (Brings out N20 from his pocket) Take, buy yourself something to eat.

AMAKA: Thank you sir. (Runs off stage) RAPHAEL: (Enter his room).

FADE

ACT TWO SCENE ONE

'Room and parlour vacancy is now displayed in front of the clinic, NURSE and DOCTOR are in the reception of the clinic.

DOCTOR: (Is reading a letter from JULIE) Julie is demanding for money, when did she go back to school? (Hiss) It is now over two months and nobody has rented the place since that mad witch packed out.

NURSE: People just come and go after inspecting the place and never come back.

DOCTOR: We prayed and sprinkled holy water in the room after she left.

NURSE: I know it works, but let us face the truth. DOCTOR: What truth?

NURSE: About the toilet, I am sure the would-be tenant will ask questions and trust people with their mouth.

DOCTOR: I will tell them what I told others. Anyway God knows we have packed the soak-away pit.

NURSE: But the problem persists.

DOCTOR: That boy Sammy was right after all it is actually the pipe that blocked.

NURSE: I feel for the new man, Mr. Raphael and his wife. But Doctor, what if the sanitary inspectors visit this premises what shall we tell them?

DOCTOR: But it will cost some extra money to repair and this people will not cooperate.

NURSE: Why not use part of the money Mr. Raphael paid for agreement to fix it and save everybody the embarrassment. Anyway, if the inspectors come, you will pay fine and still fix it. The house is yours not the tenants own.

DOCTOR: I will tell Mr. Okoye to help me call a Plumber.

NURSE: One more thing, since Mr. Raphael packed in, they have not complained despite everything and whatever we tell them to do, they do.

DOCTOR: Like?

NURSE: They pay security money early, they sweep the compound when it is their turn, something tells me they don't belong here, and they are just too decent for this environment.

DOCTOR: What do you mean?

NURSE: I cannot place them, I mean why are they here? Be careful how you deal with them.

DOCTOR: (Rising) Reminds me, I am yet to give him the agreement papers. (Enters inside)

PEACE: Comes out of their apartment, she is carrying Nne her little daughter, she goes to the clinic. PEACE: Good morning Nurse.

NURSE: Morning, how is everything? PEACE: It is Nne, we did not sleep last night. NURSE: What happened?

PEACE: She is running temperature. She kept on stooling, vomiting and crying throughout the night.

NURSE: It is the weather, there is sickness in the air. PEACE: I can imagine.

NURSE: It is N100 for registration. PEACE: (Pays) Here.

(NURSE carries the baby examines her, and enters inside the DOCTOR's office with PEACE following behind. RAPHAEL comes out from his room with a bucket of water, he is tying towel on his waist, he goes to the bathroom and enters. In the clinic, RAPHAEL's wife had just finished consulting with the DOCTOR, she comes out from the office into the reception with NURSE.)

NURSE: Just buy and use the prescribed drugs andeverything will be alright. PEACE: Thank you.

NURSE: I will ask the doctor to reduce your bill. PEACE: Thank you,you are so nice. God will

bless you. NURSE: Amen.

PEACE leaves for her room, as she enters inside, her husband comes out from the bathroom, he has a wrapped up paper containing human waste in his hand he throws it into the refuse him and walks to his room.

FADE.

SCENE 2:

OKOYE is the occupant of room 3, he come in with a Man, the PLUMBER he has in his hand a GSM Handset. DOCTOR comes out from his apartment dressed for work, he sees OKOYE and the PLUMBER.

OKOYE: Doctor, this is the Plumber. PLUMBER: Good morning Sir.

DOCTOR: Morning, show him the place.

OKOYE: (To the PLUMBER) Come. (They go to the toilet area RAPHAEL comes out to spread a rag, sees DOCTOR.)

DOCTOR: Mr. Raphael we have brought the Plumber. (PLUMBER and OKOYE have completed the inspection; they come back to the Doctor.)

RAPHAEL: That is good.

DOCTOR: (To PLUMBER) You have seen it, what do you think?

PLUMBER: It is not a small work. DOCTOR: That is all you workmen say. PLUMBER: It will cost you plenty money. DOCTOR: How much?

PLUMBER: N8,000 (Eight Thousand Naira) DOCTOR: No, No, The last person Sammy called

charged N1,500.

PLUMBER: I cannot do it for Six Thousand Naira (N6,000) (His Phone rings). Hello, yes I am in a meeting, yes I will see you later (Exit).

OKOYE: Doctor, I told you if I bring somebody from

Alaba they will charge much. DOCTOR: He is very expensive, we will look for

another person.

OKOYE: If Plumber work pays like that I might as well join them (Laughs and enter his room)

RAPHAEL: Don't mind the man, I am sure he is a contractor, he probably doesn't even know the job. (Exit).

SAMMY   comes out from outside, sees DOCTOR

standing.

SAMMY: Doctor, I greet you, Good morning. DOCTOR: What is good about the morning? SAMMY: (Taken aback) Are we quarreling? DOCTOR: I am angry with you, you refused to pay

your Vigilante Security money.

SAMMY: I am not owing, I paid six months, before my money expired, Patrick the man who lived in room 2 packed out without settling them, is it my fault?

DOCTOR: When the vigilante people ask me for money, I will bring them to your room so that you can tell them the same story.

SAMMY: Bring them now, Money, money, pay money, everything money (walks to his room)

DOCTOR: (Looking in his direction.) You will see. (Goes to the clinic.)

FADE

SCENE THREE:

It is morning, UCHE comes out of their room with AMAKA,, they head to the clinic, in the clinic NURSE is writing, as UCHE and AMAKA enter.

UCHE: Good morning Nurse.

NURSE: Morning, hope no problem, Amaka what is wrong?

UCHE: I don't know, throughout the night she kept on stooling and vomiting.

NURSE: That's no problem.

UCHE: There's problem o, I say she did not sleep last night.

NURSE: Amaka come (Checks her temperature, writes on a piece of paper, tears it out, rises, beckon on mother and daughter) follow me. (They enter DOCTOR's room) In front of room 2, RAPHAEL is carrying Nne.   Peace comes out from the bathroom. She is tying a wrapper on her chest and has her towel wrapped round her neck.

PEACE: D, this toilet issue is becoming somehow, you have to do something.

RAPHAEL: It is embarrassing, I have prayed to God not to allow anybody pack to this compound and suffer what we are suffering and I know that my God does not fail.

PEACE: That is the point I am making, change your prayer.

RAPHAEL: And then do what, fight him? The battle is the lord's

PEACE: I did not say you should fight him, since you said that no one would occupy the place till it is fixed no one has entered.

RAPHAEL: And it shall remain like that till something positive is done.

PEACE: And I believe you are the one to do something. You prayed fervently for a lot of things and I know God answers you, please change your prayer, beg God to touch him to do the toilet and let another person with the fear of God come and occupy the vacant space.

RAPHAEL: I will do that. I will not want to sin against God by refusing to pray. I will do as you asked.

PEACE: Thank you, I knew you would do it (Goes into her room)

UCHE and AMAKA come out from the Clinic and make their way to their room, they meet RAPHAEL on the corridor.

RAPHAEL: Amaka, you look dull today.

UCHE: My brother, we did not sleep last night, she vomited and stooledthroughout .

RAPHAEL: I am sure it's polluted air we breathe in this
        environment, my daughter too almost died from the same complain.

UCHE: Eh he.

RAPHAEL:	And bad water. That reminds me, I saw Amaka the other day drinking water fetched from the well, I wanted to speak to you and your husband concerning it.

UCHE:	My God, Amaka is it true?

AMAKA:	Yes ma, that day I was very thirsty, there was no drinking water and I did not have money to buy pure water.

UCHE: This city, we have no time for anything, we rush out early and come back late. God will help us.

RAPHAEL:	You will help yourself too, that time you did not have , I think you have it now, and as you can see, it is expensive.

UCHE:	It is true.

RAPHAEL: Amaka, Sorry O, get well, quick, quick.

FADE

SCENE FOUR:

It is night, DOCTOR comes out from his room with a bowl of water and starts sprinkling water on the passage, through to the vacant room, then to the clinic and back to his room, while he is doing that he is chanting and praying.

DOCTOR: Anything   spoiling   business   and preventing me from making progress depart from this house. Let this holy water pursue any demon on assignment against my work. (He repeats the prayer over and over till he enters his room).

FADE

SCENE FIVE:

Next day evening a Man in his thirties walks into the

Clinic meets NURSE reading a Magazine. MAN: Good evening Nurse.

NURSE: (Putting away the magazine) Good evening, can I help you?

MAN: Yes, I want to see the Doctor. NURSE: What for (Not giving him a chance to

answer) registration is one hundred Naira.

MAN: I am not ill, I am here to see the Doctor about something.

NURSE: Like what?

MAN: I am the head of the vigilante group in this neighborhood.

NURSE: Sorry, let me tell him you are around (Picks up intercom and speaks) Sir, there is someone here to see you, he says he

is the head of the vigilante group (drops the phone) please wait, doctor will join you soon.

MAN: Thank you (He sits.)

DOCTOR comes out from his office to meet   the MAN looking through a magazine.

DOCTOR: Mr. man, you are here, to what do we owe this August visit?

Man: (Rising) Same old Doctor (They shake hands) Good evening.

DOCTOR: Evening, please sit down.

MAN: I am here because of the vigilante money, your compound has been paying

200 Naira less than what it used to pay in the past, we want to know why, if you don't mind.

DOCTOR: I am sorry, I should have informed you before now. One of my tenants packed out about three months ago, another person has just packed in, so I will inform him and the other one...now that you are around (standing up) please come. (They both go to room 5, DOCTOR knocks. After a while, SAMMY opens the door.)

DOCTOR: MR. Man, this is the man that owes the rest.

SAMMY: Me, owing who? DOCTOR: The vigilante people.

SAMMY: I am not owing anybody anything, Mr.

Man, this I don't know what to call him has brought you to the wrong person.

DOCTOR: For 3 months now, you have not paid. SAMMY: And you have refused to see reasons. MAN: (To DOCTOR) I did not know that this is

what you brought me here for. SAMMY: I paid six months in arrears before the last occupant of room two left, the Man used to collect it and pay you people,

how am I to know that he did not pay you? MAN: That is a simple matter, you should have

sorted it out and let us know.

SAMMY: Don't mind this unserious Man who calls himself a Doctor Landlord.

DOCTOR: Are you insulting me?

SAMMY: What right do you have, bringing someone to come and knock on my door?

DOCTOR: I will deal with you o.   you blind?

SAMMY: If not for this Man, I would have showed
        DOCTOR: See, he is insulting me again.

    you my true color.   MAN: It is Okay now (To no one in particular)

MAN: It is Okay, don't quarrel over this simple SAMMY: You don't respect yourself.

        matter. MAN: This is a simple matter that should not

DOCTOR: I told him I will expose him. He does not
        degenerate to a quarrel unless there is

        cooperate in this compound.   something else
between you.

SAMMY: Excuse me, look who is talking, one day DOCTOR:
        I don't need your respect.

your cup will be full for the illegal   SAMMY: You
don't deserve it anyway.

        abortion you do in this compound, you MAN: Excuse me
(Leaves shaking his head)

        think we don't know?   DOCTOR: Your cup is getting full.

DOCTOR: (TO MAN) You hear him?   SAMMY: When it
is full, I will drink it, what can you

SAMMY: I am watching you closely.   do other than
give notice. Since that

DOCTOR: (Trying to regain control) I say you don't   woman
packed out about 3 months ago

        co-operate in this compound.   have you been able
to get another

SAMMY: How do you want me to do it by bringing   tenant?
You think if I leave this miserable small girls to come and do D and C?
        room, someone will be crazy to occupyWhen NEPA cut light, I
use my money to   it? rectify the fault. When toilet
first

DOCTOR: See, you are crazy I should have known.

developed this problem, who called the SAMMY: Yes, Staying
with you will make any Plumbers, I sweep the compound or are
        person act insane, imagine living in a house for 10 months
without toilet and it is not as if any tenant owes you, and you call
yourself a doctor.

DOCTOR;   Did I not tell you to call a Plumber after we evacuated the
soak away pit?

SAMMY: Who will pay, you want to use your trick again on me, it will
not work!

DOCTOR: This is getting too much.

SAMMY: I was on my own when you came with your trouble.

DOCTOR: (Remembers) Your rent expires this month.

SAMMY: Let it expire last month I don't care. Me I did not go too much school, but who gave you certificate, even license to practice, one day we all will know.

DOCTOR;   I should not be listening to an idiot (Exit.) SAMMY: Me too (Laughs) shameless unserious

man, your sins will bring you out. (Enters his room.)

FADE

ACT THREE SCENE ONE:

RAPHAEL is in the clinic reception sitting down, DOCTOR comes out from the inner room to join him. RAPHAEL: Evening Doctor.

DOCTOR: Good Evening, Can I help you? RAPHAEL: Yes, since I gave you my photographs for the agreement about three months ago, I am yet to see the papers, let alone sign it. DOCTOR: Am I troubling you?

RAPHAEL: No, but what is worth doing, like they say should be done well.

DOCTOR: I will send the papers to you. RAPHAEL: If you say so (Leaves to his room.)

STANLEY arrives the clinic meets DOCTOR in reception area, the NURSE too comes out from the inner room.

STANLEY is an ex-policeman, tall and well endowed in the right places, he is about 40 years.

STANLEY: Good evening Sir, Nurse. DOCTOR/NURSE: Good evening. DOCTOR: Can we help you?

STANLEY: Actually,   I am looking   for accommodation, so when I saw the notice outside, I decided to see what is available here.

DOCTOR: (To NURSE) Please bring me the keys. NURSE: (Picks it from on top of her table) Here. DOCTOR: Please follow me.

DOCTOR and STANLEY leave to go and inspect the room and they come out.

STANLEY: Where is the kitchen? DOCTOR: (Points toward the toilet) There. STANLEY: What about toilet and bathroom? DOCTOR: There.

STANLEY goes to inspect the bathroom after seeing it, tries to open the toilet, discovers it is padlocked not suspecting anything, turns around to go and join DOCTOR who has now gone to the clinic.

STANLEY: I think I like the place.

DOCTOR: (Smiling.) When will you come and pay? STANLEY: I am ready now, but...

DOCTOR: But what?

STANLEY: The broken down fence in front of the room, the torn mosquito net in the room.

DOCTOR: Those ones are no problem at all I will fix everything.

STANLEY: Where can I pay?

DOCTOR: Please come (They enter DOCTOR's inner office.)

FADE

SCENE TWO:

Opens with DOCTOR knocking on the door of room two, in his hand is a piece of paper PEACE opens the door.

PEACE: It's you, please come in.

DOCTOR: When your husband comes back, give this to him.

RAPHAEL: (Speaks from inside) Who is that? PEACE: It is Doctor (gives him the paper) he

brought this.

DOCTOR: The agreement papers. RAPHAEL: Thank you.

DOCTOR exits, RAPHAEL reads and start laughing.

PEACE: What is the matter?

RAPHAEL: This man knew what he was doing all along. (Shows his wife) see here and here, he is supposed to effect some basic repairs and provide us a toilet. He thinks he is smart.

PEACE: What will you do?

RAPHAEL: I will complete the form but I will not sign, before I do, I will let him see this.

PEACE: Something tells me he is ready to do it now, especially since we changed our prayers.

RAPHAEL: Please bring me a seat (As she moves to go inside) I have the same feeling, we shall not start the New Year like this,

something must happen (PEACE comes out with the seat) Thank you dear. (Sits down.)

PEACE: God is watching over his people. RAPHAEL: My dear, did I tell you my friend Phil won

an award in the drama category at the just concluded writer's festival.

PEACE: Really, that's great, I am happy for him. RAPHAEL: I am happy for him too and I feel

challenged to write again, you know I have not written anything since we came here.

PEACE: You and this your creative writing, since you started, it has not brought in a kobo except hope, see where it has landed us.

RAPHAEL: Are you complaining?

PEACE: Not that I am complaining but consider the future, my own, your own, Nne's too, why don't you get another Job and use writing to support it.

RAPHAEL: I thought we have already settled it that I should hang on and with faith in God, something will happen.

PEACE: I am sorry, I almost got emotional there. RAPHAEL: What would I have done without you, you are God sent.

PEACE: Darling, do you know that you are sitting on a gold mine?

RAPHAEL: Of course I am a millionaire (Laughs) how do you mean?

PEACE: You have always told me to see beauty in ugliness   have you considered the occurrences in this house since we moved in here?

RAPHAEL: It's been disgusting.

PEACE: I know, but as for me, I no longer worry about it.

RAPHAEL: (Smiles) I get the picture, I will capture our   experience   in words   as a photographer capture an image with his camera.

PEACE: You have tuned in at last.

RAPHAEL: Sure, I will tell it as it is, I will take on the theme I call. This is reality, I can see some titles already. Taken for granted.

House No.2, Dirty Game and now I think I

like this PEACE: Which one? RAPHAEL: Toilet Politics!

PEACE: (Laughs) Toilet politics, that's funny, it's

all about politics of the toilet, it has been a dirty game.

RAPHAEL: Yes, this toilet business reminds of the way politics is played in this country, the more you look, the less you see, its about promises and failure to keep promise, it stinks.

PEACE: Just thinking about it almost makes me want to throw up. Some people actually enjoy the discomfort they cause other people (Spits) tufia.

RAPHAEL: It is not as if they are ignorant of what happens in decent places.

PEACE: Are we cursed?

RAPHAEL: As a people or as a family? PEACE: Both.

RAPHAEL: Let us not go into that, as for me and my family, no curse is working on me again.

PEACE: And our lives are like this?

RAPHAEL: God himself knows why things are the way they are for us, but things are getting better.

PEACE: Well it's true, things are getting better. RAPHAEL: I believe there is nothing prayer cannot

do. It is prayer and nothing else that has kept the country together and even this family.

PEACE: I believe you.

RAPHAEL: I shall present things as they are, no additions, no subtractions, let the world see us ordinary folks as we treat each other.

PEACE: That will be nice.

RAPHAEL: As the world liveth, I will work on this

project from 13 to 15 December, I expect that by the time I complete it, this toilet issue will have been resolved.

PEACE:. I pray so, I want to share in your enthusiasm.

RAPHAEL: If it is done, then know this country can still be fixed, people know what should be done   but they prefer to cause themselves and others hardship and lack of peace.

PEACE: God will raise leaders who will put things right, leaders who will clean up the mess.

RAPHAEL: Are you telling me?

PEACE: Talking about cleaning up the mess, Sammy told me the other day that even before the toilet problem started, the Okoye's were in the habit of using the toilet without flushing it.

RAPHAEL: And yet, they blame the landlord for everything, even for what they caused.

RAPHAEL: Anyway when it is repaired we shall tackle it with the seriousness it deserves. PEACE: God is in control.

RAPHAEL: Sure, I know someone once told me that if you want to know and assess a person very well, visit his toilet.

PEACE: (Laughs) You this Man (Slaps him on the back, they both enter inside.)

SCENE THREE

RAPHAEL comes outside to spread his towel and meets DOCTOR in front of his room.

RAPHAEL: Doctor, Good Morning.

DOCTOR: Morning em, Mr. Raphael, the agreement papers (gives it to him) my wife said you complained about the toilet.

RAPHAEL: Yes, for 3 months now, I have kept quiet hoping you will do something.

DOCTOR: You know we called someone before, his fee was way too expensive, we have called another and he is already working on it, he charged 3,000 three thousand Naira, I have given him 1,500 One Thousand Five Hundred Naira, so the tenants will give him the balance, please you have to help Nigeria.

RAPHAEL: Meaning I should pay?

DOCTOR: I told the rest yesterday to gather the money when he completes the job.

RAPHAEL: It is nice to know that the work is in progress.

DOCTOR: Please try and cooperate with them

(Exit.)

STANLEY comes out from room one, he exchanges greetings with RAPHAEL.

STANLEY: Good Morning.

RAPHAEL: Good   Morning   my   brother,   how weekend?

STANLEY: Fine.

RAPHAEL: Please, I know you are not up to one week in the compound, has the landlord told you anything concerning the toilet?

STANLEY: No, the man is not a serious man. If I knew there was this problem, I would not have paid. Imagine, all the things mentioned are non-existent, pure fiction.

RAPHAEL: He copied what another fellow used for his own house and calls it agreement, just look at this, gate closes at 12 midnight, which gate?

STANLEY: I suspect   something   is not   right somewhere with the Man.

RAPHAEL: You are a Policeman, you should know.

He just told me the toilet is being fixed today, and that he expects us to pay a balance of One Thousand Naira (1,500) when the Plumber completes the work, that is three hundred Naira per tenant.

STANLEY: The man is not serious, after all I paid. He collected Fifteen Thousand Naira for agency fees when there was no agent

and ten thousand for a badly crafted

piece of paper he calls agreement. All the promises of repairing my doors have not

been kept and now this, I was not even around when it got spoilt.

RAPHAEL: Me too, but what can we do, the thing affects us all, he knows, that's why he is acting this way. Let us do it and let peace reign.

STANLEY: I don't have the money at home today after the weekend I will have something.

RAPHAEL: You are a gentleman, thank you. STANLEY: Let's keep our eyes on the man, he will

slip very soon.

FADE.

SCENE FOUR:

Next day is Sunday, PEACE and NNE come out

dressed for service, it is a full house outside. STANLEY, with a bucket of water heads for the bathroom, MR. OKOYE and DOCTOR are conversing, NURSE too is outside hanging her clothes, SAMMY is brushing his teeth with chewing stick.

MR. OKOYE: Doctor, Plumber came to collect his balance, I gave him what we have gathered but he refused, he said it must be complete.

DOCTOR: Who refused to pay? OKOYE: Sammy.

DOCTOR: Sammy, Sammy (Turns and sees him) Sammy, you again. Why did you refuse to pay?

SAMMY: Why should I pay? Every time money, the last time the soak away was not full, you insisted it was full and it must be evacuated, that's how Five Thousand Naira went, just like that.

DOCTOR: Pay your money.

SAMMY: (Not minding him) I told you the pipe was blocked and needed clearing. I looked for

2 different Plumbers who charged One Thousand Two Hundred, and One Thousand Five Hundred respectively, what did you say, it is too costly, and now

you appear with one who charged Three Thousand, tell me you think we are fools?

DOCTOR: I say complete the money.

SAMMY: For what, did you consult me before doing it?

DOCTOR: Consult you, who are you? Why should I consult you about my compound, you will do as I say.

SAMMY: When I pay you rent? Okay since I am nobody, why did you call me to pay, pay him by yourself, it is your compound.

OKOYE: Sammy, leave trouble, they have fixed the toilet.

SAMMY: Who is they? Both of you should settle him.

OKOYE: Did I do wrong by trying to make peace? (STANLEY comes out from the bathroom and goes to his room.)

DOCTOR: Leave him alone, his days are numbered in this compound. Look here boy, you will have until March ending to vacate this yard, I will send you a letter to that effect.

SAMMY: What else is new, bring it, you think I will be crazy to stay in this compound again? (Brings out Three Hundred Naira) Take, hungry man.

DOCTOR: (Collecting the money) See who is talking, don't go and look for a wife.

SAMMY: I am sorry for you, our people say you can take the monkey out of the bush, but you cannot take the bush out of the monkey, Mr. Man, if no one has told you, you stink (Fan's nose with his hand.)

DOCTOR: You are sick.

SAMMY: So are you, have you heard of this, physician heal yourself.

RAPHAEL comes out from his room with a cardboard written Flush The Toilet After Use to Avoid Disease boldly written on it, ignores the men quarrelling, goes to the toilet door and puts up the notice.

DOCTOR: (Still exchanging words with SAMMY) It's you that needs a physician, toilet disease is worrying you.

SAMMY: It's your family that is suffering from toilet disease. You know what is right and you will not do it. You think you can play on people's intelligence all the time?

RAPHAEL: (Now joins them.) Please, Please let's have some quiet here for once in this place, from the first day I entered this house it's been quarrel here, quarrel there, settle this, settle that. The toilet has been fixed abi?

ALL: Yes. (STANLEY comes out.) RAPHAEL: Why the quarrel again, why don't we

move on to the next level? SAMMY: Which is?

RAPHAEL: Maintenance, I hear before the problem people were nonchalant about cleaning up the toilet. From now, let's join hands and make sure we clean it up on rotational basis. DOCTOR: Who will start?

RAPHAEL: I will start it to set an example, I have already put a reminder there. (Points to the toilet door.)

STANLEY: I hope it works.

SAMMY: It will work if he (To DOCTOR) and his family co-operate, they like chaos they feed on sickness.

OKOYE: (To DOCTOR) please don't mind him. (holds him very tight.)

SAMMY: (Laughing) I told you. OKOYE: This life.

Two policeman comes out from STANLEY's room to join them and STANLEY points to DOCTOR.

STANLEY: Arrest him.

DOCTOR: For what (To STANLEY) but you told me you are an ex-policeman, I demand to see my lawyer.

The voice of a woman is heard off stage

WOMAN: My daughter O, the fake doctor has killed my daughter.

All of them are startled, Doctor, quickly realizing

1ST

POLICEMAN: You are suspected of illegal operation of a hospital, endangering people's life, murder, breach of contracts, environmental pollution, amongst other charges.

himself, tries to flee as Woman runs on stage and grabs him.

DOCTOR: What is it woman?

WOMAN: You will kill me too, my daughter said you did abortion for her which developed complications before she died. (She

2ND POLICEMAN: You have a right to remain silent as any thing you say will be held as evidence against you (hand cuffs him.)

DOCTOR: This is a conspiracy.

RAPHAEL: No, your time is up, this is reality, this is the end of the Toilet Politics.

DOCTOR is led away by STANLEY and the two policemen.

FADE.

THE CHAIR

*Prof. Aka The Voice, In charge of Information& Education

*Energy. In charge of Electricity, Water Resources, Oil and Steel.

*Power. In charge of finance, Security (Internal and External)

*Works.(female) In charge of Agriculture, Health, Roads & Housing

Okoro Akpan Preacher Chief Chief Boy

 Suzy

Musicians and Dancers

Crowd of Young People

INTRODUCTION

The Chair is set in a country called Jibiti. It is currently ruled by a Committee of Representatives. There is widespread Official Corruption that has led to the rumour that the Chairman will soon come. The Chairman a.k.a "The Chair" will bring change and succor to the people. Will the representatives allow it?

ACT1SCENE1:

The office of the VOICE, Prof. in charge of information and education. His office is equipped like all offices befitting officers in his position in the society. He is reading newspaper on one of the visitors seats in his office. (Knock)

VOICE: Yes? (Fans himself with the newspaper) OKORO: Good afternoon sir.

VOICE: Hmm. (Goes back to his papers.) OKORO: (Cough.) Excuse me sir.

VOICE: Yes?   VOICE: Help? I am not a money lender, have you

OKORO: No vex sir. (Hesitates.)   tried one?

VOICE: Yes young man, what is on your mind? OKORO: Oga their interest too much, even bank

OKORO: Sir, I get problem sir.   no go listen to me because collateral no

VOICE: We all have problems, what kind of   dey, dats why I come to you sir. (Almost in

        problems?   tears.)

OKORO: Big problem oga. I don't think well well VOICE: But we just paid your salary, don't you

        before I come, Sir.   have savings?

Na you by m   y only hope for help.   OKORO: Sir, I no get. Like say salary reach I for no

VOICE: En he?   dey for this situation.

OKORO: Sir, my mama dey sick well well for home,   VOICE: So if you are given the advance, what

        naimdem send for me to come.   next, Can that take care of the hospital

VOICE: And you need casual leave? Go and put   bill and sustain you?

        it in writing.   OKORO: (Thinking he is about to get the money.)

OKORO: No Sir.   No sir, E go hard sir.

VOICE: Then what do you want?   VOICE: That's true, go and apply.

OKORO: Loan Sir, like salary advance to go home OKORO: Thank you sir (Rushes off.) and see am. VOICE: (Goes to his seat, picks up the phone.) Is

VOICE: Young man, is your father still alive? That Admin, Okoro will be applying for his

OKORO: No sir, E don die, and na me be first son   salary advance, arrange it for him. Let sir. Abegsir help me.   him know that on no condition is he to request for such facility again. And draft a memo to that effect, I don't want these riff raffs disturbing this organization with their personal problems. (Drops the phone, Phone rings) Yes? Let her come in.

WORKS: (Enter Madam Works) Good day, Prof

Voice.

VOICE: Good day, Good day Madam Works (All smiles)

To what do we owe the honour of this visit?

WORKS: Haba, can't a fellow visit her colleagues? VOICE: You can, you can, welcome, please sit.

Tea, Coffee?

WORKS: No, Thank you (Pause) Prof. VOICE: Yes, always at your service. WORKS: Why are you doing this to me? VOICE: What thing?

WORKS: You know what I am talking about, the supply   of computers   to   tertiary institutions.

VOICE: Oh! That.

WORKS: Yes that.

VOICE: (Laughs) You have delivered I know. WORKS: Then what's going on?

VOICE: Don't worry, you will get the money. The cheque will be ready this week.

WORKS: Thanks.

VOICE: Em, you know, Madam Works, me too I am a human being, you know it requires too hands to clap.

WORKS: I understand, I have never disappointed anyone on that score.

VOICE: Please don't so that we can do business next time.

WORKS: Sure Prof. One more thing, what are we going to do about the coming of the Chairman.

VOICE: The Chairman? Whose Chairman? WORKS: You mean, you our information and

education representative hasn't heard about the Chairman?

VOICE: This is news to me.

WORKS: It sure is. What shall we do?

VOICE: What do they say he looks like. Who is he, where is he appearing and what has he got to offer,

WORKS: Too Many questions. No one knows for sure what he looks like, nobody knows where he will appear but we do know that he is coming in a week time.

VOICE: Is that so?

What has he got to offer?

WORKS: The people say love and hope for all. VOICE: Do we need hope?

WORKS: (Silent.)

VOICE: We don't. We the reps are rich, we ride the best cars, all the good things of life are in our disposal. Hope, the masses need it.

WORKS:	So Prof. What shall we do? VOICE:	(Silent for a while) I've got it! WORKS:	Yes?

VOICE:	Nothing, Nothing, I mean. I now

Understand that we do need a Chairman. Em what can I do?

WORKS:	Find out where he is likely to visit, and we prepare our own aspirations. Agreed we are rich, but there is no ceiling to what we can acquire, or is there?

VOICE: No. That is very sound reasoning. Leave everything to me.

WORKS:	I'll be going.

VOICE: So nice of you to have come (see her to the door).

VOICE: Now I can't wait. I'm so excited. No one knows where he is due to appear. I shall put up a press release that the Chairman will be appearing at the main auditorium in this complex next week Monday at noon (smiles mischievously.) If he fails to come, I will become the Chairman.

ACT 1 SCENE 2:

POWER is in front of his house listening to music. He is casually dressed. SUZY walks in just as POWER stands up to lower the sound of the music, turns and sees SUZY.

POWER: Hello Suzy.

SUZY: Good day the powerful man. POWER: (Embrace her) Please sit down.

SUZY: (Sits) Power Dear (POWER moves behind and caresses her face.)

POWER: Yes honey?

SUZY: Don't you think it is unsafe (Removes his hand) what if your wife sees you doing this?

POWER: No problem.

SUZY: There will be problem. My dear, why not the usual place, I will be there for you.

POWER: Sure, 9pm?

SUZY: Okay. But Power, I actually came in connection with the N200,000 for the clothes. You know I have to look good always for you.

POWER: Sure. (Reaches into his shirt pocket, gives her an envelope.) See, I was about sending someone with the cheque. I was wondering what kept you this long.

SUZY: You are a darling. I better run before trouble brews. Thanks. (Pecks him).

POWER: Feel free to ask for anything. SUZY: See you later. (Exits.)

POWER looking in the direction of SUZY. AKPAN enters through the opposite direction, coughs, POWER startled, almost falls, recovers after a while. AKPAN: Sorry Sir.

POWER: Stupid boy, I almost had a heart attack, how long have you been here?

AKPAN: I just dey come sir. POWER: You didn't hear anything?
AKPAN: No sir.

POWER: You didn't see anything.

AKPAN: I see nothing sir, I hear nothing sir. POWER: Good. The message to the chiefs, did

you see them?

AKPAN: Yes sir, they say they too will like to see the Chair, whoever he is with their eyes.

POWER: Good.

AKPAN: The whole community will be there.

FADE OUT

(Enters inside.)

POWER: What for, what do you have us the reps for? Is it not to speak for you?

AKPAN: Oga, we need change for better. POWER: Are you suffering?

AKPAN: Sir, my pikin school fee don overdue, teacher say e go withdraw am dis week if I no pay.

POWER: Too bad.

AKPAN: Oga, please, I take God beg you, help me with N1,500 make them no drive my pikin for school.

POWER: Young man, I am not your father. You know this country is very hard.

AKPAN: For us, yes.

POWER: Here, take this N1,000. AKPAN: Thank you sir.

POWER: Mind you, I'll deduct it from your salary.

(AKPAN Exits.) This meeting with the Chair tomorrow, one really has to create a good impression. I have to look good,

appear with a fine ride, and walk this way, (Walk and Stop.) He must notice me.

ACT1 SCENE3:

ENERGY: (He is in front of his garden. To himself) I honestly don't understand all this talk about the Chairman is he a spirit or what? Who is he, where is he coming from? Okay, he is appearing tomorrow with all the goodies the people hope for. Even

the people want the good things of like us. That is ridiculous (Fuming) I mean how will you then distinguish between them and us? Something has to be done.

Voice of POWER from off stage, Are you there MR. ENERGY?

ENERGY: Of Course, I am (POWER comes on stage.) Power, Power.

POWER: The Energy Man, the custodian of the resources that give us wealth.

ENERGY: Powerful man, our money and security are with you, I greet you (They laugh heartily.)

POWER: My friend, you seem to be informed about the Chairman. I know about tomorrow and some of the things he is bringing. A preacher passed by my house with another dimension.

ENERGY: Another dimension?

POWER: Yes. He said, by my understanding that perhaps we may not see the Chairman that he dwells in our hearts.

ENERGY: Then how will the people receive him. He is talking nonsense.

POWER: So all the other people will now be happy? I mean there should be people to serve men like us. We'll let them have

just enough to keep them running back for more.

ENERGY: That is true. I was thinking that

something should be done to sway the Chair to our way of thinking. Abi is he not human?

POWER: Of course he is, unless we heard wrong. ENERGY: In that case we'll make him an offer he

will find difficult to refuse.

POWER: Money, plenty of it, women, blackmail anything that will sway him.

ENERGY: We hope he doesn't try our patience enough to require trying the final option.

POWER: I hope so too.

ENERGY: Supposing, all of us reps meet an hour before 12 noon that he is scheduled to appear. That way, we can articulate our views and present a common agenda.

He has to know what our position is when addressing issues.

POWER: Fine proposal.   Let's spread   the information as soon as possible. We must protect our interest.

ENERGY: Eh-He Power, lest I forget, the N2Om deal, how far?

POWER: Not to worry, it will be well. The payment will be in our foreign accounts where no one can reach.

ENERGY: Thanks I owe you 2 fine babes. You name it. Size, Color, shape, language, you have it.

POWER: My mouth is already watery. Just get them. I will always trust your judgment on such matters any day. (Both laugh heartily).

FADE OUT

SCENE 4:

OKORO and AKPAN are the first two to arrive at the entrance of the "auditorium" the venue scheduled for the Chairman's reception. AKPAN is lighting his cigarette.

OKORO: Akpan, you with dis ciga sef.

AKPAN: O' boy how for do now? Na im I dey take console myself for dis state wey man find himsef.

OKORO: E no console nothing. Na God fit help you, no bi ciga or drink, instead problem go dey increase.

AKPAN: Okoro my broad, na true, even sef man no bi man again. I nordey fit talk for house. I dey work ebe like say I no dey work.

OKORO: Na true word.

AKPAN: I nearly beat my wife when e remind me say nothing for chop dey for house. No be her fault, na country hard.

OKORO: (Nod.)

AKPAN: She say my mate for other place them dey do well. She think say na man she been marry when she marry me.

OKORO: Wetin you come tell am?

AKPAN: Wetin you expect me to tell am. No be dis

people wey turn country upside down I

blame? OKORO: (Silence.)

AKPAN: Bros, A beg you fit borrow me N20? OKORO: You know say me with you deydi same

sinking boat.

AKPAN: Wetin sinking boat get to do with N20 to borrow me?

OKORO: Men, me too I broke, well well, make you go beg your people for accounts for I.O.U.

AKPAN: Those people? I wonder how demdey do their things for there. When boy boy like me beg for money dem go commot am for my salary, that is if dem no first of all say money no dey. But when ogadem need am, na quick quick.

OKORO: And dem no dey pay back. AKPAN: Who sai?

OKORO: Na dis our community naim I see chop- alone, greed wear cloth deywaka.

AKPAN: Why things be like dis now?

OKORO: You no know? Dem all dey prepare for retirement. So dem must grab wetindem fit before them go.

AKPAN: And dis people ready to resist the Chair wey go bring better for everybody.

OKORO: Thief thief don block their head finish. AKPAN: Dem no know say if conditions better for

everybody, dem no need to theif our money again?

OKORO: Who go come take all the big big house dem and other property whey full town? You see say change go hard?

AKPAN: True, E go hard, make we see how everything go be today.

OKORO: As dem keep us for outside, we go wait, once Chairman come dem no fit hold us back, abi?

AKPAN: Na true. 12 sharp, we go enter inside go see (Addressing the audience) and look wetin go happen today. (Start sharing leaflets to some people in the audience). "Away with Rogues" "We need Accountability" "No more to oppression"

WORKS, POWER and the Prof. of INFORMATION. Others are seated while Prof. a.k.a the VOICE is standing.

VOICE: Lady and gentlemen, before the culture people arrive, it is necessary we articulate our thoughts, so that we can speak with one voice if and when the Chairman appears.

ENERGY: That's right.

VOICE: With our common agreement, our wish will be the wish of the people.

ENERGY: Good talk.

POWER: Who shall we hear from first? ENERGY: Works.

WORKS: Why Works, is it because I am the only lady?

ENERGY: Why do you women bring sentiments into serious issues? I mean we have to start from somewhere.

WORKS: So, let us tackle energy problems.

FADE OUT.

SCENE 5:

On stage are seats arranged for nine delegates down stage centre is a table covered with white cloth. Present so far are Representatives of ENERGY,

ENERGY: What Energy problems, look be careful of your utterances (Power Failure.)

WORKS: See, I told you, your people have done it again.

VOICE: Energy, this is disgraceful. A gathering such as this and you allow for this lapse? This is sabotage, please do something.

POWER: Someone should do something before he appears.

ENERGY: Is that your voice Power? Is it not you who caused the problem, by delaying the release of fund?

VOICE: I smell sabotage.

POWER: Look who is talking, (Ignoring VOICE and facing ENERGY) What did you do with the money approved a week ago, don't tell me you've blown it.

ENERGY: Don't let us hang our dirty linen in public, Power.

VOICE: Madam Works, see what you caused. WORKS: I didn't take the light, what did I cause?

(Light comes on). No thanks to you (To

ENERGY.) It is male chauvinistic ego. ENERGY: I will not stand and be spoken to like that. WORKS: Then sit down.

VOICE: This is going too far. Works, listen. WORKS: Let me finish, you listen, inform and

educate this man since it is your job to do so, on how to behave in civil society. I am a lady.

ENERGY: You lady? Lady my foot. I don't even eat your type for breakfast. What do you expect here? Petting? We don't do that in this gathering. Meet me later, perhaps I can consider you.

WORKS: Stupid fool.

VOICE: (Shouts) It is enough (Silence) I thought we all agreed to speak with one voice.

POWER: One Voice, about what? That you all

cannot account for money given to you all to work?

VOICE: Look here, don't act holier than thou, some of us know your worth. What if the Chairman arrives and calls for a probe into the activities of this community called Jibiti are we to act the way we are acting now, like a bunch of confused children? Let us all get something right, all our fingers are soiled. We must protect each other.

(Music fades in from off stage, they freeze. Attention shift to source of music, delegates of tradition and culture, come in. Dancers and Musician lead the way, when they get to the apron, the people stop where OKORO and AKPAN are seated, action resumes.)

VOICE: Greetings our representatives of culture

and tradition. (Ushers them to their seats). Before your arrival we were articulating our various programmes with a view to speaking with one voice if he comes. Now that you are here, we can proceed.

CHIEF CHIEF: I thought you were doing just fine without us.

POWER: Not at all.

CHIEF CHIEF: I beg your pardon VOICE, what is the thing I heard about if he comes, do you have any cause to doubt his coming here today, and that we have all wasted our time and effort?

VOICE: Pardon me, (Realizes his slip.) It is a slip of the tongue; it is when he arrives, not 'if'.

CHIEF CHIEF: Thank you. Who will speak when he

comes (Silence they all look at each other) okay, Prof. (Referring to VOICE.) You will speak. Is there any objection? None. So note that we came to tell him

that we need upward review of salaries and allowances, there are more wives and children to take care of.

BIG CHIEF: Our status, apart from being recognized as first   class chiefs, we should   be addressed well. Like myself Big Chief

and my brother Chief Chief.

CHIEF CHIEF: As custodians of culture and tradition.

We do carry heavy responsilities. VOICE: Thank you chiefs for yourself vote of

confidence. I would have thought that what you will do for your people would be uppermost in your mind and not what you will stand to benefit.

CHIEF CHIEF: Come, my people know what we are doing for them.

VOICE: Alright Chiefs. Can we hear from any of you, ladies and gentlemen?

BIG CHIEF: One more thing, put it in the agenda, that weshall   require more contracts, henceforth   we want to be directly involved in the scheme of things. We are patriots.

CHIEF CHIEF: Yes, we are patriots. That was well said, how come I didn't think of it? VOICE: Who shall we hear from next? PREACHER: (Emerging from upstage centre.) Me of

course.

(All the delegates are startled, they obviously think it is the Chairman.) Why are you all looking as if you have just seen a ghost?

VOICE: (The most frightened of all the people. He least expected anything out of the ordinary to happen) Please! Please!! (Kneeling, there is general confusion, those at the apron now creep to the

stage, everybody with placards). ENERGY: Are   you   the Chairman?

PREACHER: No or do you intend making me one?

ENERGY: How come you didn't come from the front door?

PREACHER: I move as the spirit leads. My people he is

knocking at the door of your hearts, but you do not want to let him in. It is five minutes to noon, 5 minutes.

POWER: (Almost fully recovered) spare us your preaching   pastor, we all know the scripture.

PREACHER: The devil knows the scripture No doubt.

What you do with it is what matters. Jesus promised in John 14 vs 17. "The spirit of truth. The world cannot accept him, because it neither sees him nor knows him.

CHIEF CHIEF: That is not what we heard, we heard the Chairman will bring Love, hope, wealth and everything in abundance. Not truth. Shall we eat the spirit of truth?

BIG CHIEF: I wonder.

VOICE: We hear the Chairman will be filled with

Wisdom. AL: Yes.

POWER: That he will provide security for us. ALL: Yes.

ENERGY: The stress of everyday living will be a

thing of the past.

WORKS: Food will be in abundance. CROWD: (Hail)

WORKS: Hunger and disease will cease to exist. BIG CHIEF: That he will be ever ready to listen and respond to the need of the people, should there be any.

PREACHER: My people. Are you all, rich and poor gathered here today ready to make a clean break from the past? Forsake all your evil ways? All you want is comfort, wealth, food on your table without hard work. The answer to our collective problems lies in us. God sends a people the leader they deserve.

CHIEF CHIEF: Thank you. Where is he?

 PREACHER: I have played my part, to bring the good news and truth.

VOICE: (Has obviously recovered) Gentlemen (To PREACHER.) You may now leave before I call security. CROWD: (Murmuring.) No, No.

PREACHER: No Problem, if it will make you happy.

(Exit.)

VOICE: We are talking about the Chair and he is talking like someone who has high fever.

WORKS: Don't you men think there is some truth in what we just heard from the Preacher.

BOYS: (Rises.) Yes there is truth in it. Things cannot continue this way.

CROWD: We need a change. (They start chanting "Away with rogues and enemies of progress" they pounce on the Chiefs and Representatives, some flee some are floored.)

BOY: (When everything is calm.) People!

People!!

CROWD: (Respond) "POWER", all hail the

Chairman.

BOY: (Surprised) Me? CROWD: Yes.

They carry the BOY up and they all sing and jubilate as they leave the stage.

The End.